Dear Parents:

Congratulations! Your child is taking the first steps on an exciting journey. The destination? Independent reading!

STEP INTO READING® will help your child get there. The program offers five steps to reading success. Each step includes fun stories and colorful art or photographs. In addition to original fiction and books with favorite characters, there are Step into Reading Non-Fiction Readers, Phonics Readers and Boxed Sets, Sticker Readers, and Comic Readers—a complete literacy program with something to interest every child.

Learning to Read, Step by Step!

Ready to Read   Preschool–Kindergarten
• big type and easy words • rhyme and rhythm • picture clues
For children who know the alphabet and are eager to begin reading.

Reading with Help   Preschool–Grade 1
• basic vocabulary • short sentences • simple stories
For children who recognize familiar words and sound out new words with help.

Reading on Your Own   Grades 1–3
• engaging characters • easy-to-follow plots • popular topics
For children who are ready to read on their own.

Reading Paragraphs   Grades 2–3
• challenging vocabulary • short paragraphs • exciting stories
For newly independent readers who read simple sentences with confidence.

Ready for Chapters   Grades 2–4
• chapters • longer paragraphs • full-color art
For children who want to take the plunge into chapter books but still like colorful pictures.

STEP INTO READING® is designed to give every child a successful reading experience. The grade levels are only guides; children will progress through the steps at their own speed, developing confidence in their reading.

Remember, a lifetime love of reading starts with a single step!

Step into Reading, Random House, and the Random House colophon are registered trademarks of Penguin Random House LLC.

Visit us on the Web!
StepIntoReading.com
rhcbooks.com

Educators and librarians, for a variety of teaching tools, visit us at RHTeachersLibrarians.com

ISBN 978-0-593-64822-3 (trade) — ISBN 978-0-593-64823-0 (lib. bdg.)

Printed in the United States of America

10 9 8 7 6 5 4 3 2 1

MARIOKART

OFF TO THE RACES!

by Steve Foxe

Random House 🏠 New York

Mario, Luigi, Toad,
and the other racers
are preparing for a race.

They have to get their
karts in tip-top shape
to win!

Only one driver can take home
the trophy as the fastest racer
in the Mushroom Kingdom!

Will it be the brave hero, Mario?

Or Princess Daisy?

Or maybe even Shy Guy?

Anything can happen on the racetrack!

Lakitu starts the race.
Three, two, one . . .
and they're off!

As soon as the race begins,
the racers put the
pedal to the metal.
They lean into
the tight turns
and set their sights
on the finish line!

Racers have all sorts
of karts and bikes to
choose from.
Princess Rosalina chose
this kart with big wheels.

The Koopaling Iggy
chose a green machine
that bounces high
on small wheels!

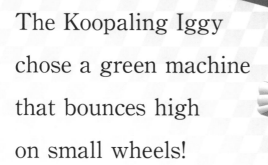

Waluigi chose
a bike so he can
do tricks.

Drivers customize their karts
however they like—then they
race across all types of terrain!

Some racetracks go upside down,

through the skies,

or even under water.

Mario had better

hold his breath!

14

Racers turn on anti-gravity
so their karts can race up
walls—and even upside down!

A racer's size can change
how they race.

Bigger racers like Bowser
take longer to get going
but have a faster top speed.

Smaller racers like Toad
don't drive as fast,
but they can speed up
much more quickly.

Items can change
the outcome
of a race
in an instant.

If Luigi gets hit with
a blue shell or a banana peel,
he could go from first place
to last place!

Finding a power-up, like
a Dash Mushroom,
can put Wendy
ahead of her
fellow Koopalings!

Some items can move, slowing down racers in other ways. Piranha Plants can chomp at the competition.

Bloopers spray ink
in unlucky racers' eyes.
It's hard to steer when you
can't see where you're going!

Once the race begins,
everyone is a friendly rival.
Even pals like Princess Peach
and Mario try their best to win.
But the race is
always in good fun!

25

Even when the competition
is fierce, everyone plays fair.

Wario may not enjoy getting
knocked out of first place
by Toad's green shell,
but it's not against the rules.
Wario will just have to catch up!

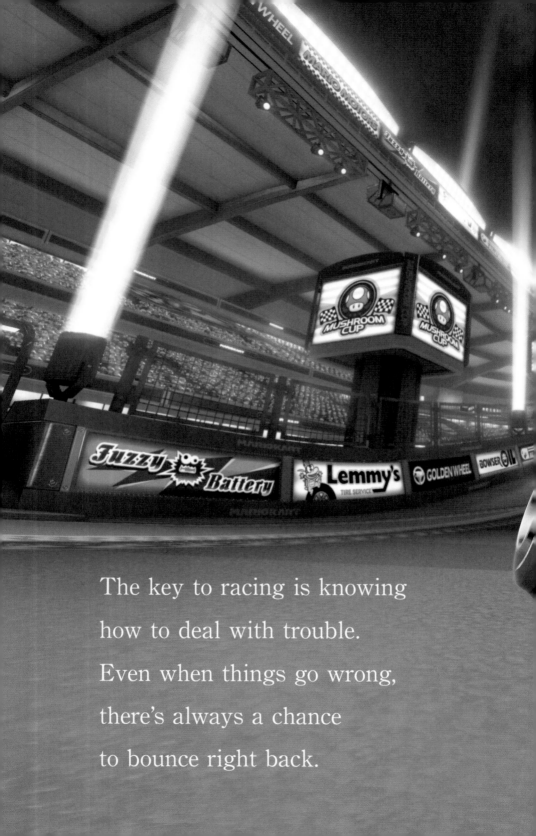

The key to racing is knowing
how to deal with trouble.
Even when things go wrong,
there's always a chance
to bounce right back.

Sometimes total chaos

breaks out on the racetrack.

It can be hard for racers

to tell if they're driving

in the right direction!

See how Mario does his best

and cuts through the pack?

The most important part of the race
isn't crossing the finish line first.
It's having fun!
Here we go!